A MUPPET™ PICTURE READER

Kermit's Teeny Tiny Farm

Written by Jennifer Dussling
Illustrated by Rick Brown

Published by Big Tent Entertainment, 216 West 18th Street, New York, New York, 10011.

 ran

up a  .

 ran

across a

and down the  .

was so happy.

He had a new farm.

 ran by .

 was putting

into the .

"I have a new farm!

A little farm!"

 called to .

"A farm! How great!"

 said.

"I will bring

a  for the

in the .

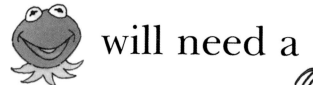 will need a

on his farm."

ran by  .

 was walking

her  .

"I have a new farm!

A little farm!"

 called to  .

"A farm!" said.

"I will bring

a  for the

that the  will lay.

 will need a

on his farm."

ran by  .

 was riding

a  .

"I have a new farm!

A little farm!"

 called to  .

"A farm!" said.

"I will bring

a for the

that the  will give.

 will need a

on his farm."

ran to his .

Then heard a

tap, tap, tap at the .

 opened the .

It was

and  and .

"Take us to the farm!"

they said.

"Here is a  for

the ," said.

"Here is a for

the ," said.

"Here is a for

the Milk ," said.

"You are all very nice,"  said.

"But I do not need

a  or a

or a

for my little farm.

I will show you."

"Here is my little farm," said .

"It is an 🐜 farm!"

hill	Kermit
road	bridge
letter	Fozzie
pitchfork	mailbox

barn	hay
dog	Miss Piggy
eggs	basket
Gonzo	chicken

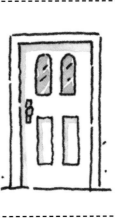

pail	bike
cow	milk
door	house
hat	ant